1700

1700

EPIC

ERIC DANIELSON

ARCHWAY
PUBLISHING

Archway Publishing books may be ordered through booksellers or by contacting:

Archway Publishing
1663 Liberty Drive
Bloomington, IN 47403
www.archwaypublishing.com
1 (888) 242-5904

ISBN: 978-1-4808-7416-9 (sc)
ISBN: 978-1-4808-7415-2 (e)

Library of Congress Control Number: 2019932002

Print information available on the last page.

Archway Publishing rev. date: 1/28/2019

To Rip

Contents

Part IV: Pont Levis

PART I
King William's War

CHAPTER 1

Mercantile Marine

Canada was French. From the Great Lakes to the Ohio Valley and on to the vast interior of the continent, France ruled. The fleur-de-lis flew from the citadel of Quebec. On the Saint Lawrence River was the township of Montreal.

Canada was ruled by department. From Versailles, the minister of marine was instructed by the Court. Several trading companies in Canada were governed by the Ministry of Marine. Seaborne trade and the French fleet were Canada's ties to continental France.

Comte Frontenac was governor-general. He received instructions from the Mercantile Marine and then executed policy. Several thousand regular troops made up the French forces in the New World. They could add numerous Canadians. Allied with the French were the Algonquian tribes of the Great Lakes and Lower Canada.

In January 1690, a raiding party of French soldiers and Indians descended on Deerfield in Massachusetts Bay Colony. Hostilities had commenced. On the frontier, one hundred war parties raided the English colonies. Comte Frontenac exercised marine policy.

I, Giorgiana Bienvegnu, was a partisan. I had access to the citadel of Quebec. My family name was good if not noble. We were the Bienvegnus. We were from Genoa. In service to France, I brought my family to the New World, and we settled in Montreal. We plowed a farm. And now we took up the firelock and knife in service of the king.

I camped and wrote of North America. The decision was whether my writing would be in English or French. It was early March as I entered the city of Quebec.

Count Frontenac asked me to sit. "Giorgiana, thank you for arriving before spring. We are at war with England and her colonies. Your service is accepted. You have influence with the Algonquian. Return in the fall." I had my instructions. I would return in the fall with my war party.

The other men and I broke encampment and filed away from the plains surrounding Quebec. It took a fortnight to return to Montreal. Surrounding the town were farms. There were also the wigwams of the tribes. "Algonquian" was an apt name for our allies. The Iroquois were our rivals, fighting with the English. Beyond the mountains were the western tribes.

I owned a farm. My brother also tilled the soil. I was also a townsman of Montreal, which had many inhabitants.

In ten days we returned from Quebec. I dismissed my war party. We would assemble again in the autumn. I returned to my brother's farm. After supper, I returned home to Montreal. I had much to do before fall.

Game was plentiful, and we trapped for fur. A bundle of fur would purchase a firelock or musket. Our native allies were armed with muskets. There were steel tomahawks and knives. Spring was planting time. And there were always commercial affairs to conduct until fall. We then would sally forth with my war party.

I employed a single servant, who was a freeman. He was not lackey or groom; he was a voyager.

I was a townsman. My house was on Market Street. I had been to school, educated by the Catholic Church. I traded furs with the tribes. By clan and tribe I was partisan, which meant war with the English colonies. We raided the frontier to extend the French domain over the continent. We contained the English to their seaboard. I had been instructed to raise a war party of Canadians and Algonquians. There were French regular troops in Montreal. I was a brevet major. Regular troops guided us in our resolve. After we assembled at harvest, we would receive detailed instructions.

I dealt in fur. The trading company paid well for North American pelts. Blankets and muskets were exchanged for fur. I was influential. My Genoese tradition brought me favor with the tribes. I acted as broker for the exchange of fur. My warehouse in Montreal shipped fur in exchange for flintlock and wool.

My house on Market Street had a pane of glass. We prospered during the winter of 1690. My dealings were honest. I acted as broker for a number of Canadians. I had influence with the tribes. I was made leader. I could count on several clans of the Algonquian. They were loyal to France. We had many Canadians among us. It was spring, and in a month would be the planting. My brother cultivated a farm outside Montreal. There would be the summer months, when we fished and hunted. In the fall we would assemble, but we would have to wait for the harvest. We would then sortie. We would be ready to do what the estate asked.

I was at home. I lived in a plank house and owned a warehouse on the riverbank. The warehouse stored fur. Caskets of chartreuse muskets and bundles of blankets were also stored there, as were steel knives, flints, powder, and lead. I gathered fur.

I sat at supper. I had a solitary servant, a retired Canadian, an old voyager. After supper was wine, and I drank. There were great evenings in Montreal. I drank. We warred against the English. The continent would be either English or French. We warriors pledged our lives. Pouring champagne, I rested. I was Mssr. Bienvegnu. I sat up late drinking wine, and then I slept.

It was noon the next day. I had been home since the summons

to Quebec. It was March 1690. I had several family members in town as well as at the farmhouse. I entertained my nephew and then retired to sit at my desk. A ledger filled the office. I counted louis d'or. When it was afternoon, I went for a walk along Market Street to the riverbank. My warehouse served as a boat shed as well.

I owned a bateaux, or barge, which was stored in the shed. We voyaged the watershed of the Great Lakes. There was also a canoe. We traversed the watershed of the Northeast. After examining my barge, I returned to my house on Market Street.

Then it was April and time to plow. Last year's pelts were shipped by sailing ships. A barque from Quebec would carry the season's fur. The barque arrived in June on the Saint Lawrence River and discharged powder and lead. There were muskets in exchange for fur. Louis d'or were also exchanged. I was well-to-do. The season's pelts would be transported to France.

I was at my desk. Transactions with the Mercantile Marine were recorded in a leather-bound ledger. I was immersed in my accounts. Equipping the Huron was in my thoughts. The English frontier reeled from the onslaught of Indian raids. That was our strategy as we contested the continent. It was this evening over wine that my servant refilled my cup. I drank sack.

Deep in my cups, I thought of the frontier. Our plowing and sowing was done. We would now wait until the harvest, after which time we would assemble.

I, Giorgiana, liked to be called Bienvegnu. I was Monsieur to the rank and file. I governed my affairs. We equipped the Algonquians. I was partisan. I led a party of Canadians and Algonquians. We traversed the Great Lakes. By navigating the watershed, we raided the frontier.

I was home. I sat over wine. I slept. The next day I was at my desk. I had a brother and two sisters.

Montreal in the summer of 1690 received a barque from

Quebec. The ship worked upstream from Quebec. The season's furs were shipped. The barque discharged cargo as well. At night I drank canary. I slept. In the morning, I sat at my desk. I worked diligently for the enterprise we had embarked on.

CHAPTER 2

New France

The extent of the Saint Lawrence River was New France. It ranged from Arcadia to Ontario. From the Atlantic Ocean to the Great Lakes was French Canada. Within this area, ten thousand Canadians thrived. With their native allies, the Algonquian, they laid claim to the New World. The continent was North America. France disputed this with the English seaboard. Our craft was called a bateaux, or barge. We sailed the watershed of the Great Lakes. We sailed Lake Ontario. The tribes were blood brothers. We were brethren of the French and Indians.

We navigated rivers and streams as our war party traveled to Pennsylvania. The winter of 1691 was the partisan raid. We scourged the frontier.

It was March of the new year. Our war party disbanded; we would reassemble in the fall. I was home in Montreal. We counted scalps. We held captives as hostages.

Home in Montreal, I sat at my desk and conducted my affairs. I administered policy for the department and the king. New France, or Canada, was a department of the French Crown. His Royal Majesty Louis XIV was sovereign. We jabbed at the English, confining them to their seaboard. It was a matter of empire.

My house in Montreal was warmed by a fire. It was a blustery March day. Our war party had taken scalps. A dozen English hostages were lodged in Montreal and were well treated. The native tribes conducted savage warfare. Jesuit priests taught civility to native warriors.

I worked on my accounts. In exchange I received goods shipped from France. I purchased a bill of lading with fur. Muskets, blankets, and steel implements were exchanged. There was an account in Bordeaux. Our trading company was on account.

I went out to see my brother on his farm. The thaw had set in. It was spring, and potatoes and corn were planted. My brother was a forester as I was. He was counted among Canadians for muster although we were partisan. My brother had a wife and children. He was told to remain at home. I was called to serve. I would sally forth again in the fall.

Equipping our allies was my chief task. Muskets, powder, and lead were supplied. Blankets and cooking utensils were exchanged. A steel knife was prized by the Algonquian. The tribes were loyal to France. They served our barter.

At home in Montreal I sat at table. A single servant was my pedigree. My servant poured my wine.

We French warred against the English colonies. The English or Americans fought valiantly defending their cabins. We suffered losses. From Montreal we struck at Virginia and Pennsylvania. In January we had been upon the Great Lakes. We traveled frozen stream and drifts to penetrate the English.

I drank coffee. I smoked. My house was wood. As previously mentioned, it had a glass window. I had a study with a kitchen and a living room. I felt indolent. I had just returned from a foray of several months. We had taken a dozen captives and were holding them for ransom. I had time to reflect. A barque from Quebec was due in June. River traffic would provision us with manufactures from Europe. We also exchanged firewood and local produce for refined goods. I was young. A colonel of regular troops advised my detachment. My war band raided on the great frontier.

A score of war parties would issue from Montreal. We penetrated the colonists' defense. It was already spring. A battalion of regular troops were stationed in the town. Clad in white uniforms with musket and bayonet, the regular or royal troops garrisoned Montreal. I set to work. The winter fur was salted and ready to exchange. I counted the pelts in my warehouse. All was ready for the summer as I calculated the winter fur. Muskets and blankets were bartered. Flints, steel knives, and glass were exchanged. The tribes were loyal to the Mercantile Marine.

It was evening. I sat at dinner, eating a venison steak with boiled potatoes.

In the town of hundreds of citizens, the garrison stood in formation. I watched the troops parade. Clad in white with colored facings, the troops leveled musket and bayonet. They were drilled in continental warfare. They had discipline. I talked with an officer of high rank. My Canadians were supported by parties of regular troops.

I was home. I ordered coffee. My servant brought me *moca*, which came from the Spanish possessions. It was approaching April of the following year. There would be the plowing and preparing of the winter fur. Cut wood was also a product.

It was afternoon. I read a book. I had a number of volumes in a small library. I read Castiglione. My affairs were in order. Among my volumes were works by Dante and Thomas Aquinas.

I looked at New France. We were a province of France. I received my orders from regular troops. We would assemble again at the harvest, which was the following week. I stored the winter's fur in my warehouse. My warehouse was full. A ship would arrive in June.

I had finished reading. I sat. It was time to go for a walk. I walked along Market Street and browsed. There was a variety of goods on display. I bought hot tea and drank the refreshment. I then returned to my house. I sat in my study and calculated our course over the previous year. We would sally again in the fall. I studied my charts. My groom attended me. It was time for dinner. In the late afternoon I supped.

There was the spring plowing. This summer another ship would arrive from France.

CHAPTER 3

The Interior

Allow me to describe North America. The continent to the Pacific Ocean embraced a region of natural splendor. In the midst of this were the Great Lakes, and rounding Newfoundland was the Northwest Passage. Canada was the northernmost area of exploration by the Europeans. In my house I defined the frontier. Containing the English seaboard was our task. Within the interior were the Mississippi and Ohio Valleys. To the southwest was Louisiana. We served the fleur-de-lis. We raided Virginia.

Sipping chocolate, I had my instructions for the fall. Our war party of three score was to ascend the Kanawha River. In my warehouse I counted fur. It was time for the spring plowing as well. I would embark with my troops in the fall.

My affairs were in order. The winter's furs were ready for exchange. There was time to rest. I sat up late.

It was morning in Montreal. I awoke at first light and breakfasted. The market was stirring. I received people in the morning. After bartering fur, I placed an order for manufactured goods. It was midmorning. I had coffee. I then went for a walk. Houses lined Market Street. I talked with a few Foresters who brought news of the Algonquian. We were in a fashion to penetrate the frontier. Containing the English to their seaboard was our purpose. Isolating their towns and cities was an objective.

I sat back. In my study I closed the books and thought of continental France. New France, as I said before, was a province. Comte Frontenac was viceroy and governor-general of the estate. The Mercantile Marine directed our effort. We had the leisure to manage our strategy. A ship from France was due in a month.

We equipped the Algonquian tribes and led their foray. We disputed the English hold on the continent. I conversed briefly with townsmen. I then continued my walk. Montreal was modest in 1691. Retracing my steps, I was home. The morning levee was complete. I sat to lunch. Cold beef and bread were served. I poured wine. With dessert there was coffee. I drank several cups.

It was early afternoon. I stepped into my study to tend to the accounts of goods and barter. With sharpened quill I registered a few transactions. My ledger was complete. The afternoon passed. A French musket was .54 caliber and deadly at seventy yards. I exchanged a steel knife or ax-head for making a tomahawk, adding in a wool blanket. In return I received the season's best fur.

It was 3:00 p.m. I drank coffee again. I smoked. My day was complete. Evening would come and, along with it, news from Quebec. A road was being cut to connect the Saint Lawrence outposts.

Riders galloped forth through New France. Some were runners I had known in France.

The governor-general instructed us. Regular troops would order our sortie. I was commissioned to provision the tribes. I was employed to utilize commercial means to do so. I had my task. Several weeks had passed. It was May. The Saint Lawrence River gleamed in the heat. It was spring. The morning bustled with traders coming and going. I had a parcel of orders bound with fur to exchange. Manufactured goods from France were bartered. In the afternoon I read. I had a journal with which to document life in Montreal.

The town bustled. War parties went forth. The English

frontier was aflame. Scalps were counted. Captives were taken. We exchanged hostages. I sat and wrote a page in my journal. I expressed my thoughts. The western tribes should be brought to bear on the Ohio River. Wampum would be exchanged. My thoughts were approved in high places. I was told to play chess. My chessboard had a number of combinations. I conceived of a series of raids at different points of the frontier. I was instructed as partisan. I counted raiding parties as the governor-general had advised me.

I drank tea. I smoked. It was a pleasant afternoon. We would sortie in the fall. My single servant brought dinner. Dusk fell. I drank wine.

[[missing pages 12-14]]

CHAPTER 4

Ontario

There was Upper and Lower Canada. The area encompassed the Great Lakes.

The Saint Lawrence River issued from Lake Ontario and flowed eastward to the Atlantic Ocean. France ruled this enclave. The Algonquian tribes were allied. The economic impetus was lumber and fur. In Montreal it was the end of summer. I had rested for several months. The frontier was ablaze. With a single servant, I received visitors and conducted business. The autumn months would see a foray. I counted Canadians, partisan, in Montreal. The tribes sallied to war. War parties raided to the east and south. The Algonquian were loyal to France.

Equipped with firelock and knife, I found that this equipment complemented native industry. At home I read. I had an assortment of books. My affairs were in order as I read Spinoza. Science was to be considered.

October would find our raiding party on Lake Ontario. We descended the watershed to English settlement. Equipping the tribes was foremost in my thoughts. The summer had passed; autumn was approaching. We sallied forth after the harvest. In these last few weeks I prepared for the foray. There was a totem with the western tribes on the Ohio River.

As I drank tea, I reflected on contemporary thought. France

was paramount in letters and art. I read Machiavelli. I was considered simple by the great. Evening fell. I would walk to the riverbank, where there was a tavern and a mug of ale. I discussed our foray with a group of Foresters. They wished to accompany me in our sally. I returned home. I slept. The morning came, early dawn. I breakfasted. Coffee and a biscuit went well together. I still received guests. Commodities from France were bartered. At noon I ate a sandwich and drank tea.

It was afternoon. I organized our foray. A war party of a score of Canadians and two score Algonquian was planned. This raiding party would descend on the colony of Virginia.

It was early September. I conducted business. It was midmorning. A .54-caliber Chartreuse musket, with mold, lead, and powder, was worth a bundle of fur. Commodities were exchanged as well. There was the market in Montreal. Glassware was valued. This was on the frontier. With a beefsteak for lunch, I drank beer. I then sat in solitude. It was the afternoon. I thought. I sat with pen in hand. New France was a province of continental France. I thought of Genoa. I walked down to the riverbank. In a shed at my warehouse was my barge. The bateaux was ready for the fall. Provisioning the craft was a task ahead of me. Our sally was aimed at the Kanawha Valley in Virginia. A number of war parties would concentrate at this point. A totem with the western tribes was our purpose.

At dinner wild rice was served. There was also a sturgeon. I drank wine. It was evening and a debauch. The next morning I breakfasted. A number of guests mingled in my parlor. I discussed hostilities and commerce. At noon we sat down to table. I saw my visitors on their way. A few were influential with the Algonquian. I sat down to tea. My servant brought me a biscuit. I reflected. There was business to conduct. The fur trade was bountiful. Fish, foodstuffs, and lumber abounded. The afternoon wore on. I went down to the riverbank to a tavern, where I had a mug of ale. I discussed our sortie. In the afternoon I was home and rested. We waged a campaign against the English.

Dinner was plentiful. I sipped wine. The evenings were a vineyard as I sat. I slept heavily. The morning came, and once again I saw a number of guests.

"Be seated, citizens," I told them.

Europe was discussed. The latest journal or periodical was a matter of interest.

At noon I was at table again. I saw my visitors on their way again. I said, "Adieu, comrades."

Montreal had a salon. I lay down to rest. A month's time would see us on Lake Ontario.

In late afternoon I sat and drank tea. The summer months were on the wane.

The tribes surrounded Montreal with their lodges, encamped in a half circle to the west of the town. This was their wigwam. I journeyed in the evening to the lodges of the Algonquian, accompanied by a trio of Foresters. It was evening as we sat around a fire. The lodge was the wigwam of the Abenaki. We smoked a pipe. I offered in exchange a number of muskets. The Abenaki looked askance at our foursome of Frenchmen. I discussed our strategy. The Abenaki gleamed with pleasure at the firelocks. The chieftain gave his approval. We smoked a pipe.

It was dusk as we returned to Montreal. It was home. My trio of Foresters dispersed. They approved of my dealings with the tribes.

I was home. I slept. The morning arrived. I ate porridge for breakfast. It was midmorning when guests arrived. We discussed hostilities. The English colonists had established a defensive mode of cabin, blockhouse, and stockade to thwart our assaults. Our policy of indiscriminate raid was being repulsed.

I read a newspaper from France. It discussed our maritime relations with Europe. I served wine. Chablis was drunk. My guests conversed in French, Italian, and English.

"Take care, mon ami." This was said. My guests left my house.

It was noon. A light wine was served. I ate lunch—a bowl of soup and bread. In the afternoon I sat in my study. I fingered a stone tomahawk the Abenaki had given me. Drinking coffee, I relaxed. I closed my ledger, which showed a balance for my undertaking. I was pleased.

The morning would see my barge launched loaded with a party of partisans. We would journey to Lake Ontario.

CHAPTER 5

The Kanawha

It was December 1691. We lay encamped on the Kanawha River in the colony of Virginia, the Kanawha being a tributary of the Ohio River. We fried venison. There was dried or parched corn to eat as well. I smoked. A day's journey away was a Miam village. We had totem with the Miami tribe. My barge was concealed on one of the Great Lakes. By canoe and sledge we traversed the colony of Pennsylvania. I was wrapped in a warm buffalo robe. Our party of Canadians included two score of Huron. We smoked a pipe.

It was our strategy to bring the western tribes to bear on the frontier of Virginia. Another pipe was smoked. At dawn we would be on our way. We sought an alliance with the Miami and Shawnee. A campfire burned. It omitted little smoke. The colonists of Virginia were mountain men and woodsmen. I examined a chart. Upstream was a blockhouse where there were Virginia militia. We traveled along a defensive line of cabins as well. We lay at a junction of a stream and the Kanawha River. The Miami village adjoined the stream. It was evening of the following day.

The fire burned. Warmly wrapped, we took turns being vigilant. Some tried to sleep. The English colonists were known to intercept or surprise a war party. Dawn broke. We packed our sledges, having stowed our canoes at a ready spot. We advanced to the Miami village, close to which we made camp. This evening would see our totem with the Miami Nation. I was Italian in the service of France. I was Canadian. We had a parley from Quebec.

We cooked a good supper. A deer had been killed. We roasted venison. A few small potatoes were added. I drank a flask of brandy.

It was dark. A party of Miami came to our camp. With two Foresters we went with them to the Miami village. There were representatives from the western tribes, which included Wyandot and Sauk and Fox. With two Foresters I sat at their campfire. A pipe was smoked. I had brought two firelocks to present to them. I mentioned fur and the king of France to the Miami Nation. Wampum was given. Another pipe was smoked.

There were a number of chieftains and lesser warriors. They parleyed with the French. They bid us to return to our camp. In camp a flask was thrust into my hands. I tasted cognac. A French Canadian said to me in Italian, "Rest, monsieur. Our mission is done."

We needed to depart. I lay down to sleep. A fire burned. Our party warmed ourselves and dozed. In the morning a mount or hilltop hovered at a height. Our party would await the Miami Nation. By a fire I drank a cup of tea. A buffalo robe was wrapped around me. It was freezing weather in the late autumn of 1691. I lit a pipe. I smoked. I enjoyed hot tea. A venison steak was given to me. Our band of Canadians and Algonquian campaigned with comfort. The Huron also lay encamped. They were given assurances by the Miami. Another pipe was smoked. I rolled up my robe and strapped it to my pack. I was wearing my long coat. I groomed myself by the campfire. I was ready for the day.

I marked our position on a chart. I clutched my musket. I told my fellow Canadians in French that we were now ready to depart at a moment's notice.

"Stay," said the Miami.

*

I stood with my knapsack and musket. I carried a half-sword, good for thrusting. I also had a dirk. In the December cold a group of Miami approached. They had fur. I issued them a dozen muskets with a mold. I also issued a case of cartridges to the tribe.

The Miami were familiar with firelocks. They needed no demonstration of loading and casting lead. They wished to have our muskets.

"Go," said the Miami.

Our party withdrew. By late afternoon we had returned to the Kanawha. We found our canoes.

[[missing page]]

We were a raiding party in English territory. We made plans to infiltrate the blockhouse and cabin system upstream. After burning a cabin and taking coup, we would return to Lake Ontario. By January we were back on the Great Lakes. In February we found my barge concealed on the shore of the lake. The party dispersed. We raised a sail and sailed to the estuary of the Saint Lawrence River. Fish and parched or dried corn were eaten. A cask of rum was broached. The wind swept the waves as we steered within the confines of New France. At the estuary of the Saint Lawrence River we camped. I counted twenty Canadians and a dozen Huron. They wished to accompany my barge to Montreal. There were no captives. A scalp was taken. We had news of the Miami.

The western tribes were tractable. I would report this to the viceroy of Canada. At the estuary of the Saint Lawrence River stood a French fort where there were regular French troops. Clad in bourbon white with red facings and with tricorn hats, a half battalion manned the fort. We were welcome. I reported to the commandant. With a salute I stood at attention. I was partisan leader with the rank of commissioned captain. The commandant of the fort was the rank of major with aristocratic epaulettes. He returned my salute.

"War party on the Ohio River."

I addressed the commandant in French.

"Bienvegnu," said the major.

I had been instructed. There was my embassy to the western tribes. I was to report to Montreal. The fort could replenish my men.

I saluted. I returned to my barge, which was moored to a pier. The barge swayed from the current of Lake Ontario. I sat in the stern. Food and a flask were thrust into my grip.

With a cloak thrown over me, I watched French regular troops mingle with my Canadians and Huron. Blankets were handed out, and a cask of brandy was broached.

"Bienvegnu," said a coronet.

"Sieur," I answered.

We were given to rest. My Huron were given cold drink and pemmican to eat. The regular troops paraded arms as my barge cast off into the main stream of the Saint Lawrence River. The current took my prow as I steered downstream. There were sets of rapids to navigate, descending the river to the point of navigation at Montreal.

My barge was back in its shed. My Canadians and Huron dispersed. De Soto, a Frenchman, would report to me in the morning. Business now presented itself. The fur trade was my concern.

CHAPTER 6

Michilimackinac

It was March 1, 1692, almost the thaw. I was home in Montreal. The first item on my agenda was my barge resting in its shed. Worn by a voyage on Lake Ontario with provisions sprung and casks broached, my barge needed repair. The mainsail had a tear. A carpenter sounded the wood. Within a month the craft would be dried and scraped. It would then be repainted. The mainsail would be patched and sewn with resin. The craft would be in good order.

In my house in Montreal I discharged my duties. My company of Canadians received a gratuity and were given to engage in fur. I had been instructed by the commandant at the fort we'd visited, and I'd fulfilled those duties. My companions would assemble again in the fall.

Our alliance with the Algonquian was made good as well. The fur trade rewarded French Canadian and Native warrior alike. Muskets and manufactured goods were exchanged. During the summer a barque from Quebec loaded the season's fur and discharged a cargo of items in exchange. I now thought of the autumn. There were the Great Lakes. Once again there would be a sortie from Montreal.

It was afternoon. I looked at a map of North America. Lower Canada adjoined the five ways in to the interior of the continent.

It was dusk. I went down to the riverbank on the Saint Lawrence, where stood a tavern. I drank a mug of ale. A number of Canadians talked with me. I enjoined them to obey the viceroy of the province. "Discipline, comrades."

"Very well, Captain."

With these comments I returned to my house. My servant served dinner of channel bass, corn, and buttered bread. Claret was poured. After supper my drinking goblet was filled. I drank until late in the evening. Drinking, I envisioned our campaign against the English seaboard. My servant put me to bed.

It was morning. A cool towel was pressed against my forehead, and I was given a strong cup of tea to drink. I munched toast. My servant refilled my cup of hot tea. A number of guests were announced. The morning passed. I received guests. The news was of France. England opposed our king. In Europe the conflict was known as the War of the League of Augsburg. In America the English colonists called our conflict King William's War. I saluted our sovereign, King Louis XIV. Orders were placed by my guests for manufactured goods. Le Havre in continental France was the port where the shipment would be received. A bundle of pelts was currency.

I served lunch. My guests ate soup. There was black bread. I poured a light wine. Meat was served. My guests bid adieu.

"We will see you again," said a departing guest.

"Farewell," I said.

It was afternoon, early March. The thaw had set in. Ice on the Saint Lawrence River melted. I drank another cup of tea. There was birchbark as an herb to sip. Spices and tea from a French Indiaman could be procured in Montreal. The weather warmed. I hired a horse to ride to my brother's farm near town. I talked with my family. The plowing would be in a few weeks. We sowed a field of corn. I returned to Montreal.

At home I determined it was 5:00 p.m. My servant set the

table. A repast of roast venison and potatoes was for supper. Wine was poured. I sat in my cups and thought of the Canadians who had come to see me this morning. They had embassy from the western tribes. The Miami and Wyandot were eager to procure firelocks in exchange for fur. They desired manufactured goods as well. Iron kettles were sought.

If all went well, then we would be at war with the English. I was settled in my cups. My servant put me to bed. I slept until dawn. I breakfasted. I then sat down to business. A ship from France was due in Quebec in June. From Quebec a barque would work its way upstream.

I was known as Bienvegnu to the governor or viceroy of New France. Our strategy was informed by royal policy determined by the cabinet members at the court of Versailles. It could be said the Mercantile Marine were involved. We executed policy. I was an Italian of good name ennobled by the King of France. We Bienvegnus had land and the farm near Montreal. We were loyal to Valois and Bourbon.

It was noon. Guests arrived and sat at table. I had a table and bench in my dining area of the house. Wine was poured. Soup was served. I cut the meat with a knife. There was bread. Afterward I was alone. Coffee was served by my servant. I drank a cup of coffee. I shuffled sheets of paper, my bill of lading for June. Fur was the primary item of exchange.

Another cargo of muskets was expected. There would be goods from Le Havre. The local market boasted native products as well. I drank coffee. I smoked. Business bustled. We were on a war footing in our province of France.

It was afternoon. I attended my family near Montreal. My brother, his wife, and our two sisters lived in a farmhouse. My two sisters were single, as was I. My brother had three children. I returned to the town of Montreal.

I decided to nap. I lay down for an hour and then went out. I walked to the riverbank and examined my warehouse and shed. My barge was drying and being provisioned. It had been freshly painted. I returned to my house. It was still morn. A small beer was served. I sat at supper that night. My servant served beef with imported rice. There was fresh corn. My servant refilled my goblet with wine. I stored a few French and Italian vintages. There was a cask of Madeira. My servant served Chablis. My simple home in Montreal saw the continental elite. My guests were a salon.

We plotted our campaigns in Europe as well as in the New World. It was evening as I refilled my goblet. The dinner dishes were cleared as I sat over my wine. As I was in my cups, my servant put me to bed. I awoke the next morning.

I drank tea and munched on toast. There was a fire burning to fend off the spring chill. I was clad in buckskins with cotton underclothing. I rolled a cigarette and lit it. I thought of Montreal. I thought of Quebec. Guests would begin to arrive. Once they did, we debated the issues at large. We considered the Reformation. I was a devout Catholic. France was suzerain. I was a simple Italian.

We conversed in Latin, Italian, and French. English was understood. Newspapers and journals from France were discussed. There was soup and meat. We conversed some more. My guests were dressed in small clothes—wool trousers and a cotton blouse. Some wore deerskin. We discussed the frontier.

Manufactured goods were eagerly exchanged. We bartered local products or fur. My guests dispersed. I was alone. My company was good. I needed time to contemplate what business there was. I was entrusted with solidifying our alliance with the Algonquian. Goodwill was essential to this endeavor.

It was afternoon. I walked down to the riverbank and had a mug of ale. I conversed with Canadians. I returned home and napped. At supper there was salt junk and vegetables. I drank wine. The table was cleared except for my drinking cup. I sat over wine. Canary was poured.

I sat up late. I imagined the thrust and parry of an Indian raid. I went to bed. The next morning my servant held a cool cloth to my forehead, and handed me a strong cup of tea. The tea revived me. There was housekeeping to do. Guests would arrive at 10:00 a.m. We cleaned house. My desk was in order. I'd received bills of lading. My guests arrived.

*

It was an April day in 1692. The house was polished and in order. The washing was hung up on a line behind the house. Guests arrived.

I served cold champagne. An officer of the French Royal Army exclaimed, "Mon Dieu!" The officer was a subaltern. I poured Portuguese wine.

We conversed in French. I said, "We have a few vintages."

"Our royal troops supplement native and partisan troops. They have discipline. We travel light and with speed."

"Captain." This was said by the subaltern.

I mingled with the other guests. Some were Canadian. A few citizens of the town associated with one another. It was lunchtime. Soup, bread, meat, and wine were served.

Later I sat alone in my study and smoked. A chart or map of the Great Lakes was spread before me. I noticed Michigan. Our outpost was Michilimackinac. Our subaltern had excused himself and left. It was evening, and we had our instructions. Our autumn foray would be to the site so named. It was in accord with the fur trade.

It was morning and I breakfasted. My servant poured a mug of hot tea. The French Mercantile included French Indiamen.

CHAPTER 7

1696

A number of years had passed. The English colonists had withstood our onslaught during that time. There was a lull on the frontier. It was 1696. I was home. Business concerned me. Across the sea in Europe, there was a truce. King William and Queen Mary ruled in England. I was preoccupied. My affairs were good. The Algonquian who had been repulsed by the English colonists were armed with modern firelocks. Trade was good. In Montreal I continued with our salon. A number of women visited. Newspapers and journals were still discussed. Wine was served.

My servant attended to matters. I was Canadian. My brother and his family continued to grow crops on our farm. I and the troops raided the English. Regular French troops manned our outposts. We trafficked with the Algonquian. Our good king Louis XIV reigned from Versailles. We were a trading company to France. Upper and Lower Canada were provinces of our king. I need not mention Colbert and his influence on Canada. Mercantile theory promoted our commerce.

It was morning. My servant made breakfast. Coffee was poured. I breakfasted and drank coffee. I was a veteran of so many evenings in Montreal. There was toast. I smeared jelly on it. Home currencies were made in the town.

It was 9:00 a.m. A few guests arrived. By 10:00 a.m. the parlor was full. We made conversation, speaking in French and Italian. We discussed the French fleet.

"Our Mercantile Marine is based on maritime policy." I said this with an amore in Italian.

There was a Canadian, a pupil, and a Dominican who were interested in economic theory. This Canadian was also a Tomahawk in our partisan warfare.

"We are a trading company, provincials," I said.

The conversation went on. Latin was spoken.

The Catholic priesthood was primarily Jesuit, with a few Dominicans. They taught God and civility to the tribes. They taught higher education as well in Montreal. Our priesthood was a sedate influence on the Algonquian.

It was afternoon. I drank tea. Chocolate was also served. There was tobacco. I sat down. My desk was organized. My ledger was exact. We awaited a ship from France. A barque upstream was our tie to Quebec.

Drinking tea, I mentioned that a French Indiaman had tied up in Quebec. There was also commerce from Le Havre. I examined my reports. Our warfare had met with bitter resistance from the English. We would campaign anew.

I thought of our salon. A number of ladies and wenches were guests.

We discussed fashion, which was entering Montreal. I was dressed in corduroy fashion. I wore a linen shirt. Madame pointed out luxuries for me. Madame mentioned small comforts. I no longer drank in my cups. I would retire early and sleep.

In the morning I had a cup of tea. I smoked. My tobacco was Turkish. The English popularized the Levant. My servant served dinner. I had coffee afterward. I went to sleep early. In the morning I had a strong cup of tea. My servant knotted my cravat. Dressed, I donned a light coat. It was early morning as my guests arrived. A light wine was served. We discussed Greece.

Newspapers and journals found their way to Montreal and were read and discussed. Convention was observed. Descartes and Spinoza and the English Isaac Newton were discussed. Copernicus from Poland was mentioned. Madame arrived. A number of women entered my house. I mentioned the Jesuits to Madame. Madame was M. Chalon of Lyons.

From Lyons she mentioned Burgundy and the river Rhone. I expounded on Genoa. Madame was critical of me. She mentioned a farm near Montreal.

"Captain, a provincial."

"Madame."

I thanked her for her presence at my house.

M. Chalon sipped tea. It was jasmine from Madras, India.

M. Chalon mentioned the church and manufactures. We discussed trade. I swore fealty to Louis XIV. The Grand Monarch fielded 414,000 regular troops to oppose the Dutch and English. A division of this array was assigned to Canada. M. Chalon was interested in our salon. To rude and coarse Canadians she was known as Le Femme. She sipped tea. She mentioned Toulon. Our conversation was understood.

Lunch was served, broiled venison and a bowl of soup. Corn bread was also baked. The assembly dispersed. I was alone with my servant. I also had an aide assigned to my rank. The aide was a regular French officer.

We harassed the English frontier. I was partisan. The fur trade was good. We equipped the Algonquian. I sat down. I asked my servant for a cup of tea—black tea from Bombay.

Moodily I reflected on our civilization. French art was patronized in the province. The ladies were good, but we men reflected on war. The continent was our goal. My servant served sandwiches and retired for the day. The afternoon wore on. It was getting to be May. On the wall of my study was a map. North America was our quest.

CHAPTER 8

1700

We were Canadians to Les Belles, France. A number of years had passed. I had graduated from our salon to roistering and gaming and drinking at the tavern. The Saint Lawrence River was the riverfront.

Le Femme enjoined us to be single men. Some took orders in the church. I was thrown to my own devices.

I was a Forester. I coauthored a war party in our struggle against the English seaboard. My rank was partisan. At the tavern on the river shore I met a number of boatmen whom I could enlist in our foray against the English. There was a parley on the frontier. Peace was enforced.

The Jesuits taught college in Montreal. I had a diploma from their college. I could teach unlettered provincials. I had ceased to drink. At the tavern was a mug of cider. So many voyagers! I could use them in time of war on my barge. We discussed trapping fur as well. We observed during our raids on the frontier that the Algonquian needed discipline. I enforced authority to native tribesmen.

I returned to my house. My servant was getting old. I was forty years old. My servant poured coffee. I smoked. My going to the tavern was my own effort to mingle with rough-cut Canadians. The voyagers were an economic impetus to my enterprise.

Muskets were raised. Harrying of the English colonists was carried out. Loyalty to our king was paramount. Canadians fell into line. The Algonquian sang and did a war dance. In these times there was commerce with France. Imports to Canada were valued. Our ladies of Montreal were an influence on rude men. They were listened to. I drank again at the tavern.

A knife and steel ax-head made a tomahawk. These were worth fur. A musket was worth a number of furs. I sat in my den at my desk. My affairs were well conducted. My warehouse was worth louis d'or. I wore buckskins. The ladies dressed me in linen.

I sat and drank. Beer was plentiful. I had a clear head. So many Foresters were subordinate to me. I conversed in Italian and French. I was at the tavern again. There were maidens serving ale. *Base* was the word. Indian blood was also discussed. I drank a tankard. There was a truce with the English. Regular troops imposed the peace. The Algonquian were given to hunt.

A game of dice was played. I abstained. Barter or trade was discussed. I talked with a maiden. The English slang for one like her was *moll*. *Prima donna* was said in French. I offered a louis to pay for the rounds and then departed. I returned to my house. A cold plate was supper. I drank tea.

Soon our salon met at another house. A regular officer presided. He was an aristocrat. My charts and calculations were of interest to him. I was said to be ribald. There was also finesse. I joined Madame Chalon.

"I have means and affluence. I am alone."

Madame Chalon replied, "That is well." She also said, "Bienvegnu, you are of use. Continue. You are given partisan rank. Regular troops enforce the king's authority. Obey."

I sipped a glass of wine. Soon I took my leave.

I was home. I frequented the tavern. Great was the work assigned to me. The French Mercantile Marine ruled our province. I set to work. The fur trade was my task. I served our king. There was a lull in hostilities. Supper was a lake trout. There was rice. My servant poured coffee.

In the evening I was sober-minded. Commerce was good. I spent the day at my desk. Our salon was patronized by regular officers. Madame Chalon was my friend.

Hostilities were not relaxed. There would be another effort. The Algonquian prepared.

The next day, my servant pressed a dry cloth to my forehead. I sipped a strong cup of tea. M. Chalon had returned to France. Another madame took her place. I was encouraged in my solitary existence. *Be composed.* I devoted myself to our cause.

The morning passed. I closed my journal. I sat at lunch. Soup was served. My servant poured wine. This afternoon would see a walk to the market in Montreal. I had a rendezvous. In the evening I went to bed early. I awoke at first light. There was work to do. A ship from downriver was expected with stories of the frontier.

I sat at lunch. A bass was served. There was a potato. Squash was also served. My servant mentioned he was a domestic. This was true. I sat at home that afternoon. Authority ruled in Montreal. In a home near the market was a maiden whom I knew. As the decade closed, she and I were wed. In January of AD 1700 our issue Henri was born.

PART II

Malplaquet

.

CHAPTER 9

New York Town

My name is Leslie Esperier. I am an English subaltern assigned to the New World. My pals were killed at Oudenaarde. I was sent to New York Town. The French wars engulfed the American frontier. We opposed the French in Canada. My regiment were the fusiliers posted in the colony of New York. I joined my regiment.

Garrison life was good. I was told to mend myself. A mug of ale and a beefsteak was my vice.

There was porridge for breakfast. My uniform was neat. I wrote letters home. We drilled. As coronet I commanded an element. My troop in line stood well. There was ambuscade. We faced the foe.

In camp I had a tent. There was a cot and a chair to sit. I had blankets. My kit was in good order. We were posted to New York Town and were billeted in a home. I had a bed. Formation was held in the square. I settled to writing letters and reading a book. A mug of ale was my vice.

In 1701 the French and Indians had been repulsed at Schenectady, New York.

It was 1708. In New York Town the inhabitants were loyal subjects. The colonists were Americans. The town was located on Manhattan Island. The Hudson River emerged from inland waters. Albany or the Dutch Fort Orange was upstream. In this sphere was a confederation of loyal Indians known as the Iroquois.

My regiment of fusiliers was posted to reinforce colonial levies fighting the French. The French and Indians warred over New York Colony. Stationed on Manhattan, I drilled my troop. We were confident that Americans could oppose the enemy. England supported its colonial levies.

I wrote letters and read books. I was told gaming, wenching, and drinking were to be shelved. I was told to behave. I calmed down. Dice had gone with my dead friends at Oudenaarde. I could make a fresh start.

My room was neat. My uniform was pressed. With halberd, I paraded my troop.

With the Americans and Iroquois we faced the French. Fusiliers were light infantry.

We taught marksmanship with a Tower musket. After drill, I would return to my room. I wrote letters home. I had friends in England. Things were well.

I had campaigned at Blenheim and Ramillies and was now on a new assignment. I was reformed. I had taken being a rake-hell and a daredevil too far. I was penitent. I solaced myself. The Esperiers were of noble blood. A cousin was a peer. The family were Baronet.

I was given to discipline. My troop drilled and paraded.

My fusiliers were told to stand in rank. Expertise with the Tower musket was demonstrated. There was porridge for breakfast. I inspected my men. At noon was salt beef and a biscuit. I drank hot tea.

At my desk I wrote letters. I described the colony of New York to a friend in England. My notes on America were well received in London. In the evening I sat with a fellow officer, passing the night. A violin called a fiddle was played. I slept. I awoke in the morn. I drank a cup of tea. I spent the morning drilling my troop.

Formation was at noon. I allowed my men to be dismissed for lunch. Salt beef was cooked. There were also biscuits. Coffee was boiled. After lunch the men fell into formation again.

I dismissed my men. I returned to my quarters to write letters. Later I posted the letters.

It was 4:00 p.m. An ale in a tavern was in order. At 6:00 p.m. I sat at dinner. The evening passed. The next morning I awoke and drank hot tea. We had orders for Fort Orange on the Hudson River. Albany was a town.

The march would be on foot. I had a small sword and a muzzleloader pistol. I also carried a pike. Skirmishing was our trade in the British Army. Her Majesty Queen Anne ruled. We were loyal to the queen. Marksmanship and skirmishing were the order of light infantry. We faced the French and Indians.

Her Majesty's colonies were our trust. To the devil with the French.

I awoke the next morning with hot tea. My kit was packed. On the march I took a spare uniform and shirt. I had a razor.

It was early light as the march began. A wagon train followed our column. The regiment was in order of march. A corduroy road skirted the Hudson River. The march continued. By noon we were abreast of the Hudson. The march would continue.

A company of colonists protected our advance and our wagon train. The regiment continued. It was late afternoon. The baggage train held our rations. The next morning the advance continued. We were well on our way to our post. Fort Orange protecting Albany was an embattled fortalice, a stockade with an earthwork. It boasted cannons. Albany was a town at the point of navigation. A road was cut. We continued our march.

A party of Iroquois was seen. They, with the company of colonists, protected our column. It was the afternoon of the fifth night of the march when we arrived at the point of navigation on the Hudson River. We could see Fort Orange. It had been a Dutch or

English rampart. Albany was a cluster of houses forming a bourg. Our regiment filed onto the town common.

Our colonel commanding the regiment thanked the colonists for screening his fusiliers.

"Thank you, Americans, and the Iroquois."

Our regiment paraded inside Fort Orange.

An American general with a company of militia had defended the outpost. French and Indians menaced. Albany was fortified.

The regiment was given quarters to camp. There was a barracks in the fort. I had a room. It was small. There was hot water. I bathed, and then I dressed in my spare uniform and shirt. I shaved. Teeth were important, so I used a toothbrush.

I attended the colonel. He reported to the American general. The general said he could use a British regiment. I saluted.

"The Second Fusiliers," I reported.

"Defending settlements and skirmishing with French and Indians," the general said.

"I want a company posted to the rampart."

It was supper. A venison steak was served. There were potatoes. I drank cider. There was corn and peas.

The next morning, the French and Indians raided the outskirts of Albany. Musketry answered them. My troop manned the fortalice.

At supper beef was served. There was corn. I drank cider.

The next morning we manned the parapet. The French and Indians were in earnest.

CHAPTER 10

The Hudson

It was now several years later on the frontier. English troops had learned Indian warfare. I was a veteran of colonial war. We had repulsed the French and the Indians.

Assembled at Fort Orange, we returned to New York Town. A Maryland regiment relieved our troops. I was posted to New York. My friends in England were interested in my notes on Americans. I was glad to oblige. I had a room in a house on a boulevard in New York City. I limited myself to a few ales. My letters home were full of details of the American frontier. I described the French and Indians. The French disputed our seaboard. Containing us to the Atlantic coast was their intent. They controlled the interior. They marshaled the Algonquian, a foe to Iroquois, or other tribes friendly to the English. We stood fast with the Tower musket.

In New York City I settled down with Americans. In 1712 the colonies were mostly rural. There were only a few towns becoming cities, such as Boston, Philadelphia, and Charleston. Of course New York City was included. In Florida were the Spanish. England had seized Gibraltar. I was in my room in New York. I wrote letters.

The Second Fusiliers were detached to the colonies for the duration. I was assigned to New York City. Queen Anne's War continued. In Europe, with the victories of John Churchill, Duke of Marlborough, peace talks were in the making. In Europe hostilities had been called the War of the Spanish Succession.

I was liaison between British and colonial or American troops. The Americans' equipment was entrusted to my task. I conducted affairs. A regimen was enforced. Colonial troops required discipline. In New York City the bourg was becoming a major port. Trade from overseas was introduced. At lunchtime I attended a business luncheon. Manufactures were also in the city.

Parliament regulated commerce. The topic of stimulating trade was introduced. At lunch I attended a meeting. Manufactures were regulated.

It was afternoon. I drilled militia. Colonial troops were competent equipped with Tower muskets, steel knives, and tomahawks. I directed colonists to stand in formation and at attention. My American sergeants obeyed me. The troops stood line of battle. I dismissed them.

It was evening. I sat at table and ate beef. Later, until it was time to sleep, I sat in a parlor and conversed. I was a British officer loyal to Queen Anne. I saluted Her Majesty. I viewed the colonists. I liked Americans who were also loyal to Her Majesty. I introduced etiquette to many.

I was told to sit. I listened. I was asked to share my ideas. I slept. In the morning I drank a hot cup of tea and ate a biscuit. later my colonists stood in formation. We practiced drill. My sergeants were veterans. I taught them cadence and to wheel left.

At noon the troop fell out to cook lunch. Rations were provided. The men would reassemble in the afternoon. At 1300 hours the troop stood in formation. They were dismissed. With the afternoon free, I wrote letters. I posted them in New York. There was a mail packet to England. I also received letters.

It was evening. I sat at supper.

We were forming two regiments in New York. I established their tables of organization. The troops drilled. We discussed the peace. Envoys were meeting at Utrecht. There was a cessation of hostilities. There was quiet on the American frontier. I was confirmed in rank and stationed in New York City. My observations of colonial life were of interest to those at home in England. I continued to muster two regiments. I taught them to stand in line. With leveled muskets, they would have a volley.

My troops were good. In homespun with crossed belts and tricorn hats, my men paraded. My friends in England had influence. I was promoted to captain's rank. I listened to the men's concerns. They were subject to the mother country. I enjoined strengthening the frontier. The French and Indians were a threat. I made my men a reserve of two regiments in New York City. Some of the men were New England muster.

News came from Europe. It was 1715. Queen Anne had died. There was peace. In England the succession went to the German house of Hanover, of Stuart blood. Parliament instructed us. I kneeled.

George I would ascend the throne. We swore fealty to George I. God save the king.

I had a room in New York City. At my desk I made notes on our American colonies. There was peace. We had gained territory in Nova Scotia and Newfoundland. I drilled our two New England regiments. Were there hostilities, the two regiments could stand in line. Actually the colonies could raise tens of thousands of troops. On the frontier we could use a few thousand. The French and Spanish were our foes. My two New England regiments were a model of continental warfare. There was peace.

I noted American agriculture. Most colonists tilled small farms. These farms each had a cabin and a shed. Corn was planted. There were small gardens as well.

There were a number of small cities. Urban life went to a few thousand colonists. I wrote letters home. The colonies and their interests were debated.

The Piedmont in Virginia was the frontier. The mountains were sparsely settled. In New York I sat at parlor at night. The University of London was discussed. I was offered tobacco. I rolled a cigarette. I smoked. Wine was served. I drank a cup of tea.

"Thank you," I said.

The next morning I marshaled my two line regiments. They served as a model of regular troops. I lunched at noon. At 1:00 p.m. my troops were dismissed. The men were encouraged to look to their equipment. They wrote letters home. I received mail. Friends in England were charmed by my American notes. In a tavern I had a single ale. Back in my room I pressed my uniform. I was complimented by the colonel.

CHAPTER 11

The Common

It was 1715, the Peace of Utrecht. The Royal House of Hanover was ascending. I was loyal to George I. We kneeled to Parliament. It reminded me of having rights. The rights of Englishmen were espoused. In the colonies Americans were free-born men. This was the spirit of the colonists loyal to George I.

In New York City I dismissed my men. My troops could stand in line. It was afternoon. In my room, I was clad in summer dress. I penned my notes. I was giving our seaboard my observations. Rice and tobacco were grown. The labor was demanding in the southern colonies. Fishermen and ironmongers flourished. There were a number of seaports along the Atlantic coast. Commerce flourished. Shipbuilding excelled. The colonies' population was under a million inhabitants. In common we were loyal to the English Crown.

Wearing a frock shirt tied at the throat, I sat at my desk. My notes were enclosed in a linen package to mail to England. It was afternoon. Donning a light coat with my captain's epaulette sewn on the shoulder, I walked to a tavern for an ale. I discussed regulations with the men at the bar. Regulation wasn't liked. I explained on a greater scale the concerns of local manufacturers. I was listened to. By Parliament we kneeled to George I. Our monarch was of Tudor and Stuart blood.

The tavern bustled. After having a single ale, I departed, first paying for the beer with a shilling. I was back in my room. It was almost time for dinner. A family gathered at supper with guests. I was a guest.

A beefsteak and spaghetti was served. There were boiled potatoes. Wine was served. I sipped a mug of cider. I buttered bread. I was a British regular officer. My task was to train two American line regiments. Give it a year and I would deploy them in continental warfare.

The father of the family with whom I was staying beamed at me. I was his guest. The father's name was Lefebvre. To the family I was welcome. In the evening we sat on a sofa. I listened to music. The newspaper was discussed. There was peace. Lefebvre was a colonel of militia. I could advise him on his muster. He was cordial.

I described the continent and French regular troops. Lefebvre was impressed by discipline and savage warfare. The evening passed. I retired to my room. I was up the next morning and wrote letters. I sipped tea. I ate a biscuit. In uniform, I paraded my troops. Two colonial line regiments impressed British regular officers. In formation I drilled the colonists. Discipline was enforced. My sergeants were mastering the drill. The formation stood in line. I dismissed the troops and then retired to my room. I had letters to post.

Over a single ale once again we discussed Parliament. Commerce was booming. Men of affairs discussed the laws governing them. The colonies were loyal to George I. We kneeled. At supper I sat with Lefebvre. The colonel of militia was quartermaster. We discussed logistics. I was an infantry captain.

We discussed two line regiments of colonists. The British Army was interested. Clad in light blue, paid a few shillings, and fed, my two line regiments stood in line of battle. I drilled my troops. They were taught to level and to receive a volley. My sergeants fell into formation. They drilled the troops.

It was evening in the parlor of American colonel Lefebvre. There was a piano to listen to. I sipped tea and soon fell asleep. In my room, I awoke at first light. A hot cup of tea with a biscuit was served. Freshly shaved, I stood inspection. My uniform was neat. I inspected my men. Grizzled with drooping moustaches, the men passed inspection. Bathing was encouraged. Fresh underwear and clean shirt was enforced. Two line regiments stood in formation. I dismissed the men.

I wrote letters in the afternoon and posted them to England. Over a single ale I discussed politics. In the tavern we discussed the rights of man. Loyalty to our king was fierce. Enemy espionage was interested in subverting the English Crown. I described the French, the papacy of Avignon. Such was the fleur-de-lis. I mentioned our opposition to the pope.

I was home. Supper was served. We had spaghetti. I finished with cider. I sat in the parlor, and we discussed events. French and Indians were the foe. Regular troops disciplined colonial levies. Once again I described the French, this time to Lefebvre.

I had a groom who set out my shaving gear. I shaved with a razor. After dressing in clean linen, I donned clean clothes. My uniform was neat. Following my preparations for the day, I drank a cup of tea. I breakfasted.

It was after breakfast that I inspected two line regiments. The men stood in formation. I read the king's Articles of War to the troops. My two regiments were dismissed. I had the morning to post letters. I stopped for coffee in a café and then returned home. Beef was served for lunch.

I was interested in the American colonies. They might prove to be a bulwark to the English Crown.

CHAPTER 12

1720

Years had gone by. I took ship to England. We arrived in Hull on the coast of England. The Esperiers were gentry in Suffolk. I took horse to my older brother's estate. I was still the rank of captain. My epaulette was sewn on my uniform coat. My brother lauded me.

We discussed America. I told him Americans were not to be oppressed.

"They are a very individualistic breed of fighters, but loyal subjects," I said.

My brother gave me advice on the conventions or service to the king.

I spent six months at a house in Suffolk. I had my instructions from family and friends. I had money too. I took ship to the Port of New York. I rented a small house near the harbor. I had a valet. With the rank of captain, I was given to be undersecretary to a British colonel. My pen was of value.

As a clerk I copied orders. I also wrote letters for the less literate. A bluff major told me, "You are versed, Esperier."

I was up early in the morning. I drank a cup of tea. Morning found me at an orderly room. I copied orders. At midmorning I had coffee. Resplendent in my scarlet coat, I put pen to paper.

Senior-ranking British officers mentioned my two-line regiment of colonists.

"We are raising regiments of colonists to be Royal Americans," they said.

Senior officers found me interesting. I had my pen.

At lunch I ate salt beef. A mug of ale was served.

In early afternoon I was dismissed. I had my own time. I was home working on a manuscript. My *Notes on America* was already in manuscript form. A printer in England was interested. He had the manuscript. I mentioned the French and Indian War.

I went out later. A British colonel thanked me for my observations. I was of use. I returned to my house. My valet, who cooked for me, sewed my clothing, and served as my groom, was home. After breakfast I found myself in an orderly room again. I copied orders. I was free to go after lunch. Beef was served. There was ale. I had the afternoon to explore New York City. The town had grown.

The harbor bustled with trade. Ships were anchored in the harbor. The city boasted manufactures. Iron foundries poured steel. On the outskirts was countryside. Dairies were seen. The forest met the countryside. Indian raids were known to occur. In this panorama was the continent that either France or England would rule.

It was 3:00 p.m. I was home. My valet groomed me. He trimmed my close beard and moustache. I dressed in a clean shirt. He served me a glass of wine. I drank claret. I was a young bachelor of age. I had been in rank six years.

It was peacetime in the colonies. Socially New York City boasted Dutch pedigree. I was enjoined to be a member of staff. Religious services were on Sunday. My family was Whig.

George I was our king. I kneeled to Parliament. The House of Hanover ruled.

Whiggamore were the English liberals. My family, like I,

was Whig. It was the next morning. I awoke to a hot cup of tea. My valet groomed me. Dressed in uniform, I was staff. I copied orders. The orders were signed by a chief of staff. At lunch I ate salt beef. There was a glass of ale. It was afternoon. Once I was dismissed, I walked through New York City. The city bustled. I made purchases at the market.

At home I sat in my study and read a novel. My notes were being publicized. My valet served sherry. I drank wine. It was evening. I sat at dinner. My valet served ham with yams. Yams were American produce. I had chocolate for dessert. Coffee was served. I smoked. Tobacco and squash were colonial produce. Cattle were raised there too. I slept.

My valet groomed me the next morning. I had breakfast. There was tea. I went to work. My pen copied orders. A British colonel was chief of staff. The colonel said, "Esperier, you have come of age. Give it a year and rank."

I said, "Thank you, Colonel." I saluted.

I copied orders. I also maintained a ledger. New York City flourished. I liked to watch the harbor. A group of British officers were resident in New York. We stood and toasted the king. At home I worked on my notes. There was a revision. My observations were liked.

The next morning I made tea. The day passed. When it was evening, I dined at home. My valet poured wine. I had letters from home. My life in America inspired interest at home in England. I read Cervantes.

The next morning, I groomed myself and drank tea. At work my pen was busy. The chief of staff signed my cursive. I was dutiful. For lunch was salt beef, our ration. There was a mug of ale. It was 1722. Long live our king.

CHAPTER 13

1725

It was the year of our Lord 1725. I had been in rank eleven years as captain. In New York City a colonel informed me that I was brevet major. I was assigned to staff. I drank a cup of tea. George I ruled. We toasted the king standing.

"Major Esperier, you will do. Report back tomorrow." I went home. (I still rented a house by the harbor.) My valet served wine. He added an epaulette to my left shoulder. I donned my uniform coat and stood with sword. My valet poured claret. We drank the glasses down. My valet congratulated me.

My duties would include being undersecretary to the chief of staff. I did not mention that I was a graduate of the University of London. I had become a baccalaureate.

Dinner was served. A Newfoundland cod was for dinner. There were also vegetables. My valet poured canary. We drank.

"A glass," I said.

We toasted the French and then the Spanish. I retired to sleep.

The next morning, my valet thrust a hot cup of tea into my hands. I groomed. At headquarters with the British staff I was given a desk. I settled into my duties. Morning passed.

"You may go," said a colonel.

I walked through New York City. I had letters from home.

"Congratulations," one of the letters I'd received read.

I was rank of major.

It was for clerking that General Staff could use my talents. I was known for a book. My *Notes on America* was read.

Socially I was single. The staff ordered me to retire. I was alone in my house. I had a servant. My valet had served in the Lowlands. It was afternoon. Enjoying the summer, I sat with a sherry. Reading absorbed me. Defoe was a favorite author. When evening fell, I sat down to dinner. Our ration was beef. There was claret.

The morning found me at headquarters. I clerked. I was making observations on our English colonies. I reflected. Empire was voiced. The English ruled possessions of imperial proportion. The French and Spanish were mortal foes. I made note. I described the interior of the continent and the Great Lakes.

"You may go." This was said by a fellow major.

I had the afternoon off, so I walked through New York City. At home I sat at my desk. My pen was busy. I liked Americans. The afternoon wore on. I had a sherry. Royal Americans were being recruited. I remembered my two line regiments. I sat at supper. Braised beef and rice were served. In the evening I read a volume by Bunyan. The next morning I drank tea. With the day to myself, I spent it shopping, buying provisions in New York. I was brevet major. I talked with people at the market. Once at home, I stowed my purchases, sat down, and poured claret.

I penned letters. I had correspondence. Evening came. I dined alone and then drank coffee.

I must mention our king. Enemy espionage surrounded our monarch. Parliament ruled. I was loyal to George I. Standing, I resumed my coffee. I considered the enemy and sat. Morning found me at headquarters. I clerked. My pen was employed again. I was staff.

Luncheon found me at a café, where I ordered beef. I was

given the afternoon. Once again I strolled through New York City. The French in Canada were a merciless foe. I collected books. I read a few titles. My house by the harbor was extant. I could see commerce on New York Bay. Within the city were manufactures. I was staff.

I spent the morning copying orders. There was also correspondence. I was employed. Time was given off. I had leisure. There was time at home. My valet took my uniform coat.

"Esperier. You are well-grounded." A colonel said this to me.

"You may go," a major said to me.

I shopped. At home I drank tea. It was early afternoon. I went out and later returned home. I sat at dinner. I liked cider. There were also a few apples. I sliced cheese. My valet was attentive.

"I served under Marlborough and Eugene." This was said by my valet.

"Stand by," I said to him.

A week passed. We toasted our gracious king.

In New York our troops penetrated the French military. The staff studied Canada. I was given time to reflect at home.

CHAPTER 14

1728

I had visited England again. A number of years had passed. There was news. George I had died. Long live his son George II. I was English staff in New York City, the colony of New York. Our staff made contingency plans on Canada. I was busy with my pen.

The colony was in honor of the House of Hanover, George I, and George II. I also wrote notes on the French. I was home. I rented a house on the harbor. The city bustled. Seagoing ships discharged their burthen. Outgoing ships took on cargo of local produce.

I walked through the city. British headquarters was in downtown Manhattan.

An office suite held our staff. I had a desk. There was a lounge. Behind closed doors senior officers debated strategy and New France.

I clerked. A team of undersecretaries were subordinate to me. I documented a British Army senior staff. In our cabinet I forwarded a copy of our strategy to Whitehall.

Once at home I relaxed and drank claret. In my study I made note of Georgia. Oglethorpe was a name. I dined. My valet poured tea. I smoked.

[[missing page]]

The French were imposing. France was the dominant power in Europe. Canada bristled with defenses. The Canadians' onslaught with savage tribes made them feared. In New York City our British staff gave French Canada a look. English regulars were poised to engage the French.

George II was king. We stood and toasted the king. It was morning. I sat with staff. I led a drafting room of clerks and scribes. At noon I ate beef and drank a glass of ale.

"Esperier, you may go."

I was home in my study, where I drank claret. Soon I dined. A New England cod was served. I tasted cider. In the evening I was alone. I read. Ben Jonson was good. I also read Francis Bacon. There was much to learn. In the morning I drank a hot cup of tea. I was in dress at headquarters. I had bathed. My shave was clean. In fresh linen I stood inspection. I was at ease.

I spent the morning assembling our intelligence on Cape Breton Island in Canada. At coffee break I instructed my young officers. We worked until noon. Beef was served, along with a pint of ale.

In the early afternoon we continued with our plans. We had assembled a strategy for countering the French. I was given posting instructions. The General Staff in England reviewed our work. It was 1500 hours. I could leave the office.

At home my valet poured Madeira. I sipped the wine and sat down. My valet took my uniform coat. I was in my shirt and trousers. I rested. The next morning I drank tea. At headquarters I copied a document. We probed the French interior. "At noon you may go" was said.

I walked through the town and went home. There was a cluster of houses where I lived. My valet served sherbet. It was cool. Sitting, I lounged in my study. My desk held two rough manuscripts. With pencil I made notations. My valet served wine. I was busy.

In the early afternoon I rested. I had penned several letters to England. I posted them. Dinner was a beef rag. Rice was served. Brandy was poured. After dinner I smoked. I took paper and tobacco and lit a cigarette. It was evening. Candles were lit. I read.

In the evening I read Voltaire, The next morning I drank tea. I groomed for the day. In breeches and stocking with shirt, I donned my uniform coat. I walked to headquarters, where I directed members of staff. At midmorning coffee I smoked. We were busy through noon. Lunch was served. Beef was our ration. Beer was drunk. We had a deadline at 1500 hours. Then we were dismissed.

I was home. My valet had me sit. He served wine. I stood. George II was king. I bowed to Parliament. In the evening I went out. I had met a number of people socially. I went to dinner. Having known disappointment romantically, I was a bachelor. I went home to read a book. Rabelais was representative of French thought.

In the morning I drank a cup of tea and then groomed. I was given the day to post letters and write. In my study I sat at my desk. France the nation-state was our foe.

CHAPTER 15

Notes on the French

My notes begin with "The Song of Roland." Roland fell in the Vale of Roncesvalles. From this is the line of the ancien régime.

I sat at my desk. Another year had gone by. I was thirty-nine. My rank of major had been confirmed. I was assigned to staff. I had time to write. Georgia, the thirteenth American colony, impressed me.

My family in England were well. They corresponded with me. I wrote letters to friends as well. In New York City our contingency plans were done. We had been British staff. The General Staff and Whitehall had been advised.

The French aimed at the continent. Our seaboard of Americans was under assault. I rested. In the morning I would be reporting to work. We recruited Americans. I continued with my *Notes on the French*. Marseilles was their oldest city. That evening I sat at my desk. I had a nightcap before sleep. I awoke the next morning. I dressed. There was a cup of tea. I walked through the town and was at headquarters.

I was busy all morning supervising a team of young officers. We were employed to counter Canada. We had resources on the frontier. Our fleet was aimed at the Saint Lawrence River. Whitehall had our intent.

Once I was home, my valet served wine. I relaxed. I had two rough manuscripts. I penciled them.

In the fall of the following year, George II was king. I still read. Books absorbed me. I took an interest in our colonies. I had a view of the continent. I sipped wine.

I had news from England. Friends wrote. We debated the conflict in North America. There was lively thought. It was morning. I drank a cup of tea. I dressed. I spent the morning sitting at my desk, where I read letters. My correspondence occupied me. At lunch salt beef was served. I drank ale. There was cheese.

I lounged in the afternoon. Our staff had a complete set of plans. I made note. The Gironde and Garonne were rivers in southern France. I examined my manuscripts. It was early afternoon. I reflected on the year. France was formidable. I sipped a glass of wine. The next morning would see me at work. Dinner was served.

In the evening I read. Dr. Johnson was popular in certain circles. I would retire early and arise before dawn.

I awoke. My valet thrust a hot cup of tea into my hands. I washed and groomed.

My valet served lunch. There was a rag of beef and some cider. A glass of claret followed. There was cheese. I sat in my study, examining my two manuscripts. I made notes. The Champagne was a French vintage. I smoked. Cigarettes were becoming the fashion.

I sat back. In breeches and shirt, I wore slippers. I donned my coat. I asked for shoes. I went out. I had posted letters to England. My correspondence was good. Back home, dinner was served. The next morning I was at headquarters.

"Esperier, you may go."

I returned home. The harbor bustled. I ordered tea. My *Notes on the French* was taking shape. *Oglethorpe* was my second manuscript. Georgia was founded. I sat at lunch. Salt beef was served. A light wine was poured.

It was afternoon. My rank of major was confirmed. I was staff. I sat at dinner. I sipped sherry.

[[missing page]]

CHAPTER 16

Oglethorpe

It was 1729. I was thirty-nine years old. My thoughts dwelled on our thirteenth colony of Georgia. The colony, with penal attributes, was sponsored by a gentleman named Oglethorpe and was in honor of the House of Hanover.

The Spanish in Florida were in opposition to the colony. They raided the southern proximity. Southern tribes that were warlike also raided the efforts at agriculture in the confines of the settlement. Savannah was the capital town of Georgia. George II was king.

In New York our staff made preparations for war with France. A hostile peace was enforced. I was home again and had been commended for my work. A duplicate copy of our contingency plans had been retained.

"Esperier, you will do."

I drank claret. I was wearing slippers. My valet filled my glass. Dinner was served. Manhattan clam chowder was served. I sipped wine. Indolent, I stood up. Dinner was over. I retired to my study, where I looked at my finished manuscripts and made notes. Mountains encompassed northern Georgia. I relaxed. Candles burned. I doused them and went to sleep.

The next morning at headquarters I was told off. "Esperier, you may go."

Staff was standing down. We had completed our work. I strolled home, where I sat in my study. I read. Defoe was good. There was also Swift. It was afternoon. There had been salt beef for lunch. A colonist sat down. He had news of the harbor. I poured wine. The colonist accepted a glass, and we discussed commerce. Coffee was then served. The colonist left.

I sat alone. The French were making preparations to renew the conflict. We had proof of this. I was in my study and read. The New Testament interested me. There was ancient Greece. I was called to dinner. I sat down in the dining room. A roast was served. After supper I was back in my study. A history of England interested me. I made notes.

The plains of Georgia were savannah.

I went to sleep and awoke the next morning. At headquarters we were being reassigned. I received my orders. My appointment to staff was being confirmed in New York.

"Esperier, you have the makings of a good staff officer. We retain you."

I went home. In my study I looked at my two finished manuscripts.

Staples in Georgia were rice, tobacco, and indigo.

I sipped wine. Having been posted again to New York City, I needed to make new arrangements with my valet. I needed a housekeeper. I was rank of major, staff. Dinner was served. I ate a yam. Cider was poured. I smoked. I added tobacco to my routine. I went out. Lights glowed. It was night. I attended a social occasion.

At home I slept. I awoke the next morn. Hot tea was served. I had the morning to myself, so I wrote letters. After luncheon I posted my letters. My correspondents included southern colonists. I had letters from them to document my notes.

I relaxed and sipped wine. In the evening a fire burned in the grate. I slept. Morning came. I drank hot tea and then dressed.

The business suite that held our staff was closed. I was ordered to remain in proximity. I had work to do. I knew the colonies, and this was useful, the staff had told me. Senior-ranking British officers liked my knowledge of the New World.

I was home. Coffee was served. I smoked, rolling my own cigarettes. The morning passed. My valet looked to my uniform. I was clad in small clothes. Afternoon came. I drank wine. It was an autumn day in the colony. After supper my candle burned into the night.

PART III
Vauban

CHAPTER 17

Henri Bienvegnu

I am Henri Bienvegnu.
It was 1740. I was forty years old. Bienville had asked me to sail with him. I declined the offer because my family was rooted near Montreal.

I was a French regular officer, rank of captain, Le Royale Armée. I attended the Jesuit college in Montreal and earned a BA degree. My field was logistics. I had a desk in Montreal. I was married with two children. My wife was a belle dame.

My father, Giorgiana Bienvegnu, was killed in ambush in 1710. I have a half-brother from my father's liaisons. His name is Half Huron. He is a warrior of Huron descent.

I have seen maturity. Hostilities with the English had simmered since Utrecht. I was a French officer.

As mentioned, I had a desk in Montreal. The town had flourished since the beginning of the century. In the city, the old town of earlier years had been preserved. In my father's house I sat at my desk in my study. I maintained a set of books. My wife had a house servant to assist her. My two children were at study and sedate.

Spain had a Bourbon King. In France Louis XV was being crowned. The regency had produced a grandson to Louis XIV.

I was in uniform, clad in white trousers, linen shirt, and white coat. The coat had scarlet facings. My hair was combed and curled.

I powdered my hair. As a gentleman and an officer I had a sword. I sat with a pen. A half regiment was stationed in Montreal. As quartermaster, I was attached. The Mercantile Marine governed Canada. I had trade relations with them. Canada was a province of France. I was a citizen as well. Quebec and Montreal were towns or cities. The provinces boasted a population of tens of thousands. Control of the interior was our concern. The English were expanding their seaboard. Partisan warfare still dominated our strategy. This was our struggle with the English. The Algonquian were our native allies. We warred over the colonies.

In Montreal I sat at my desk. I had accounts. Furs were our major export.

A cousin owned our family farm. Crops were also used as exchange. Imports were manufactured items. Weapons and lead were procured. The tribes were equipped to wage war. Steel implements were exchanged for furs.

I had a degree. Some thought imagination was needed in limited resources. I thought of expanding our export. Ships from France were commercial ties to Europe. Montreal was at the head of navigation on the Saint Lawrence River. Barge or canoe or portage was our avenue to the watershed of the Great Lakes.

I was absorbed at my desk. As a military officer I could see strategy in commerce. New France boasted eighty thousand provincials. France mustered thousands of Canadians. I thought of New France since Utrecht. Our provinces had grown. The regency since 1715 saw the coronation of Louis XV. I knelt to our king.

Hostilities had simmered since the peace. English expansion or settlement characterized the frontier. Our strategy from the Mercantile Marine was a policy of containing the English seaboard. A number of forts had been posted. At strategic points were fortresses. We continued to raid the English. Partisan warfare was waged.

A division of regular troops had been assigned to Canada.

French regular officers disciplined partisan Canadians. Savage warfare ruled. A number of officers protested the excesses of the Algonquian. Jesuit priests were among the tribes teaching civility. Wild game, corn, vegetables, and fur were items of exchange to the French.

Firelocks and steel items were exchanged to the tribes. I enjoined humanity to the English. I was not unheard. With these reflections I sat at my desk. The year was 1742. I worked my accounts. Items of exchange were sought. Barter was exchanged for currency. The Bienvegnu were a clan near Montreal. Our family had grown in the last few years.

The family farm produced a crop of corn and wheat. In my home, my family were at their tasks. I worked in my study. In early afternoon the house relaxed. I sat at dinner and talked with my wife. Ships from France unloaded at the riverfront. Warehouses with the season's fur discharged their products to be loaded aboard the ship.

I managed accounts. At work, I reported to a senior-ranking French officer.

"Thank you, Bienvegnu," said Colonel Despain.

I returned to my house.

I sipped wine. It was getting to be fall. The Saint Lawrence River saw traffic to Quebec. There was a viceroy in that city or town. We obeyed. I had my instructions and was promoted to major. The rank was brevet. I saw a season's fur go aboard the ship. There were items of exchange.

The Mercantile Marine governed Canada. Exploiting the fur trade was their intent.

I went to dinner. Supper was served. I conversed with my family. Wine was poured. In the evening I thought of New France.

[[missing page]]

CHAPTER 18

Louisbourg

Cape Breton was an island that controlled the estuary of the Saint Lawrence River entering the Atlantic Ocean. The Gulf of Fundy was the geographic term. A star-shaped fortress modeled after Vauban's frontier fortifications in France was built. Louisbourg stood as a rampart controlling the entrance of the Saint Lawrence River.

Constructed in honor of Louis XV, the fortress commanded the Atlantic approaches to French Canada. It was a number of years later in Montreal. I sat at my desk. A Vauban fortress was planned in disputed territory south of Lake Champlain in New York Colony. Located on Lake George, the fortress was named Ticonderoga. A smaller fortalice was built at Crown Point.

Partisan warfare continued on the frontier. The Algonquian were French allies in opposing the English. I was made busy in maintaining contracts and ordering manufactures from France. Local resources were also used in procuring materials. As quartermaster I oversaw procurement. Trains of goods were transported to the lakes and the site of construction.

A half regiment was stationed in Montreal. I reported to the commandant in town. Life was pleasant. In my father's house my wife and children were at home. The children studied math and languages. My wife supervised the house and sewed.

I was at my desk. My study had shelves for a number of books. Months had passed. There were rumors of hostilities with the English. Partisan warfare was our assault on the English frontier. The Algonquian were our allies. Our intent was to contain the English seaboard. War parties formed.

As the structures on Lake Champlain formed, regular troops were posted on Lake George. In New York Colony the Iroquois Confederation was hostile to the French. Indian raid on the Saint Lawrence was known. I viewed our enclave in the New World. Our strategy involved the Mississippi and Ohio Valleys.

A number of years had passed. Louisbourg stood as a rampart on the Atlantic estuary of the river. In garrison were regular troops. The regiments boasted cities and towns of France. Our outposts in the region were our strategy. In New France we prepared for a continuation of war with the English.

In my household I was at my desk. Our construction was concluded. Louis XV was His Royal Majesty. I kneeled to our king. The Bordeaux regiment marshaled in Montreal. As rank of major, I stood aloof of formation. Dressed in white breeches with linen shirt, I wore white stockings and my uniform coat. The commandant reviewed us. I spoke in Italian and French. I wore a dress sword.

An Indiaman had moored at Quebec. Barges and lighters brought its cargo to Montreal. In my house my wife had boxes of tea. I drank jasmine. I sat. The Mercantile Marine was interested in commerce. Trade with India and the Orient was promoted. It would seem our reverses in the War of the Spanish Succession had been decisive. However, a Bourbon king in Spain, and our interests in India, had succeeded. The victories of Admiral Suffren counterbalanced defeat. Trade was promoted.

Our commerce on the Saint Lawrence River flourished. I was home. I looked at our strategy. It was 1745. Our outposts and fortresses were being provisioned. Regular troops formed at vital points. I drank tea. I smoked. Tobacco was an herb the Algonquian knew. I continued to work. Exports were a concern, as was procuring supplies for regular troops.

The season's furs had gone aboard ship to Europe. I wrote letters at my desk. The house was tranquil. In summation I could give you an idea of New France. The provinces were Upper and Lower Canada. Quebec and Montreal were fortified. It was thus that hostilities approached. Partisan warfare was engaged.

I was home. In the lull of disquietude that had been, I was with my wife and children. My desk was busy. My office handled imports and exports. Montreal was a port. My task was logistics. I thought of New France. I was instructed by the Mercantile Marine. There was a viceroy in Quebec.

I thought of Louisbourg. The fortress commanded the approaches of the Saint Lawrence River. Our defensive measures were good. Our offense was Indian raid and privateers at sea. The reign of Louis XV approached. In France the regency was over.

Personally I felt pride in my country. France was Catholic Majesty. At my desk I worked on accounts. The season's fur was ready to transport. It was thus that hostilities ensued. There was a French and Indian raid.

CHAPTER 19

King George's War

Royal Governor Shirley of Massachusetts Bay Colony called for an expedition against Louisbourg. It was the spring of 1745. New England was aroused. French privateers anchored under the guns of Louisbourg raided New England's commerce.

Ships were gathered. A force of New England muster was assembled. They sailed against Louisbourg. I am writing these words as Cape Breton lies under siege. The English armament was impressive. The defenders of Louisbourg stood against the force of New England.

[[two missing pages]]

French regular troops defended the fortress. The citadel had been provisioned to withstand a siege of some length. The English called this new conflict King George's War.

I was home. Montreal was on a war footing. An Algonquian encampment lay outside the city of Montreal. The Algonquian wore paint. My half-brother Half Huron was in the encampment at Montreal.

With my half-brother I smoked tobacco.

Half Huron mentioned the Iroquois. The six tribes of their

confederation were foes. My half-brother led Huron warriors. They were loyal to France.

In the colonies, to our understanding in New France, there was an Awakening. Baptist and Presbyterian ministers avowed to awake. New England was in ferment. In loyalty to George II, they sailed against Louisbourg. I cannot tell you of these months. Louisbourg was isolated, its supply was severed, and it was short of water. The besieged were forced to surrender. Louisbourg had fallen.

New France was stunned. The approaches to the Saint Lawrence River were in English hands.

On the frontier, Indian raid was fomented. The frontier simmered. It was of no avail. Our ties to France and the Mercantile Marine by sea were severed. Peace ensued. In Montreal I resumed my tasks. I was with my wife and children. On my desk were bills of lading of the season's fur. I awaited the peace. I thought of the interior of the continent. The Saint Lawrence was isolated.

Lower Canada embraced the Great Lakes. The Saint Lawrence River emitted from Lake Ontario. The Mississippi River rose to the west and flowed to the sea. In this geography was Louisiana. Cartier, Champlain, and La Salle had laid claim to these regions. Savage tribes claimed land in this midst and were bonded to France.

I was thinking of the Great Lakes. Our outposts were positioned in these regions. A bitter peace came. Territory in Nova Scotia and Newfoundland was ceded to the English. Louisbourg was returned to France.

On the frontier partisan warfare ceased. A truce was enforced. At home in Montreal once again, I had shipped the season's fur. I was at my desk. Our preparations of prior years gave us credence to the interior. We strengthened Louisbourg.

New France bloomed. With the plow, crops were sowed, and wild game was plentiful. It was the spring of the following year.

I had my accounts. Ships had returned to the Saint Lawrence River. It was a shadowed peace. Savage warfare had cast a pall over disputed regions on the frontier.

I was at my desk. It was the summer of the following year. We languished in defeat. Our defenses were in repair. On Lake George stood Ticonderoga. On the isthmus to Lake Champlain stood Crown Point. On the frontier were outposts. The interior was firmly in control of France.

Once again we contained the seaboard of the English.

At my desk I worked on provisioning regular troops. The magazines of our fortresses were filled. Quebec and Montreal were provisioned. I was made busy procuring foodstuffs and manufactures. Commerce had returned to the Saint Lawrence River. I saw the season's fur embark again. The continent would be either English or French. The conflict must continue.

Restoring the confidence of the Mercantile Marine was in order. Our commerce was intact. I worked at my desk. Once again I thought of France. Exports and imports were good.

The French fleet remained intact. Once again our commerce flourished. I was at my desk. I maintained accounts. Logistics was my field. In afternoon I would open a book. Reading a novel was of interest.

The summer waxed. Armaments were procured from Europe. I was indolent. I sipped wine. There was cheese. We had learned a lesson from the previous war. It was a lesson to be learned.

CHAPTER 20

Braddock

A number of summers had passed. It was the early 1750s. France laid claim to the Ohio and Mississippi Valleys. This claim was disputed by the English. The border of the colony of Virginia was the Ohio River. The colony of Pennsylvania also extended to the Ohio River. France disputed this claim.

It was thus that our strategy was to unfold. The French and Indians enforced our claim to the Ohio Valley. Engineers had visited the site of an outpost. A fort was to be built on the waters forming the Ohio River. Construction completed the fort. It was known as Fort Duquesne.

[[missing page]]

An emissary from Virginia registered a protest. This was from Royal Governor Dinwiddie. The fort was completed and garrisoned with partisan and French regular troops. There was an outcry in the English colonies. Fort Duquesne was unacceptable. I write of this while gaining age. Once again hostilities simmered. We awaited what the English would do.

It was the spring of 1755. A brigade of English troops had been dispatched to Fort Cumberland, Maryland. Their commander was General Edward Braddock, a European professional. French and

Indians could not face disciplined troops. Braddock proposed an advance on Fort Duquesne. Engineers could cut a road.

Formed in column, the British approached Fort Duquesne. Partisan warfare ambushed the column. The brigade was shredded to the last man. Braddock was mortally wounded. Colonists and the wagon train survived.

The savagery of the engagement shocked regular officers. The action was deplored in France.

I sat at my desk in Montreal. Canadians were not well thought of. Hostilities once again resumed. The Ohio River and Lake Champlain were the focus of conflict.

Once again I was busy at my desk. I maintained accounts on the commerce of New France. Provisioning troops was one of my tasks. Traffic with the Algonquian was another. The season's furs were waiting to be transported. We awaited France.

A decision was pending in Europe. It was 1755. There was news on Lake George. French regular troops were defeated. French Baron Dieskau had engaged New York colonist Johnson. The French were defeated. Because of this morale suffered in Canada. Lake George was the center of conflict. French forces rallied at Ticonderoga and Crown Point. While I was sitting at my desk as 1756 approached, His Royal Majesty made a decision. His two leading generals were Montcalm and De Saxe. Montcalm would command Canada and the New World. Montcalm was humane. He was also gifted.

Montcalm was entrusted with the defense of New France. He was civilized. The Mercantile Marine was informed.

I was home, working at my desk. My family were secure. My children had grown. They were young adults. The Jesuit college in Montreal was considered. I talked with a Jesuit. The focus of the conflict was Lake George. There was also Lake Champlain. The two lakes were at the headwaters of the Hudson River. This was

Ticonderoga's importance. I was quartermaster. I was employed. My wife too had aged. She was a dowager.

Montreal was a town or small bourg where commerce flourished.

[[missing page]]

I made use of local products. There was a foundry in Montreal. Powder and lead were produced. Our supply of manufactured goods was limited. Commerce existed by way of the French fleet. Our seaborne commerce was extant.

As the year ended, the focus was the Ohio River and Lake George. Indian raid was fomented by partisans. The eastern shore of Lake George was English. Regular troops were deployed. Winter set in. It was 1756. General Montcalm arrived in Quebec. The Marquis de Montcalm prepared to take the field.

It was March. The thaw set in. Ticonderoga had been reinforced.

CHAPTER 21

Ticonderoga

It was 1758. The fortress stood on the western slope of Lake George. The fleur-de-lis flew over its ramparts. The fortress commanded the region forming the headwaters of the Hudson River. On the eastern shore an army was forming under the command of General Abercrombie.

Abercrombie was a political appointment. He plunged into the disorder that was entrusted to him to get into shape. English colonists were part of his force. Thousands of English regulars were added. Ticonderoga was their objective. There was discipline. The complaints were many. Abercrombie was not dull.

He set his soldiers to work building whaleboats to transport his army on the lake. They gave him mobility.

The forest was filled with French and Indians. They harassed the English.

Abercrombie proposed a frontal assault at Ticonderoga. The English regulars were being indoctrinated in forest warfare. The English colonists were being put into line. Companies of Rangers engaged the French and Indians. I will not be the judge of Abercrombie. He wasn't liked.

As the summer solstice arrived, Abercrombie delivered a frontal assault on Ticonderoga. Along the opposing shore the French had built a stockade. The English were pinned down by the abatis. Their force was repulsed. French regular troops manned the stockade. In defeat Abercrombie was informed that Montcalm commanded at Ticonderoga.

Once again the English Army, low in morale, was encamped on the eastern shore of Lake George. Discipline was enforced.

I was in Montreal with instructions from General Montcalm. I was quartermaster. My accounts included provisioning the troops posted on the lakes. Cartridges were also provided. Pack trains supplied the troops.

There was news. Louisbourg had fallen a second time to Amherst and Wolfe. It was my responsibility to organize a supply train from the Saint Lawrence to the lakes. Mules and pack horses bore their burdens over forest trails.

Montcalm commanded at Ticonderoga. A lesser fortress was situated at Crown Point. The enveloping of Abercrombie's army was being enacted. Amherst was the new appointment to face Montcalm. The rival armies held their positions on Lake George. Disorganized by defeat, Amherst's army was recovering its morale. May I say Amherst inspired respect?

I now document news from Europe and the Far East. The English had formed a coalition with the king of Prussia. In the lowlands an English Flemish army opposed France. Frederick, King of Prussia, was fighting a stubborn defense against rival powers. England supported him.

In the Mogul Empire of India, French forces opposed English commercial interests. In Montreal I recorded the situation on Lake George. Companies of Rangers recruited by the colonists opposed French and Indians. Amherst drilled his army into line. He advised caution in assailing Ticonderoga. Isolating the fortress was his strategy. His whaleboats commanded the lake. Montcalm's strategy was to envelop Amherst. The campaign had become the topic of romance. The rivals were Amherst and Montcalm.

On the high seas were still the French fleet, a fleet in being.

Commercial ties with France had been severed with the fall of Louisbourg. I was employed on my accounts. Logistics was my field. A system of roads had been cut through New France. From these roads forest trails supplied the lakes. Ticonderoga boasted heavy cannon. This was an engineering feat. In Montreal I was abreast of news from Europe. In India, French and English interests opposed each other.

CHAPTER 22

Quebec

French regular troops were stationed at Ticonderoga. With French and Indians, their task was to envelop Amherst. Amherst's strategy was a standing army on Lake George. With this he meant to isolate Ticonderoga.

Montcalm was capable. Returning to Quebec on the fall of Louisbourg, he opposed Amherst and Wolfe. I was stationed in Montreal. The war continued on the lakes. I sat at my desk. News from Europe was good and not good. Frederick, King of Prussia, continued to defy the continent.

The presence of the French fleet continued to open commerce to the New World. It was the French fleet that sustained the Mercantile Marine. My task was import–export. New France boasted manufactures and products from Europe. I was rank of major. I was quartermaster.

[[missing page]]

My task was to provision and equip the troops at Quebec. General Montcalm and Governor-General Vaudreuil instructed me. Partisan warfare reverted to the lakes.

My brother Half Huron was a chief opposing the Ranger companies on Lake Champlain. My brother warred on the

English. In Montreal I organized the produce of the province in our war effort.

Powder and lead were produced. There were forges and foundries as well. Montcalm continued to oppose the English. Partisan warfare continued.

In Montreal my son and daughter continued to study at the Jesuit college. My wife had aged. In her late fifties, my wife was a dowager.

I had earned my degree. My children knew the Greek classics. I had discussed their education with a Jesuit.

I was employed at my desk. I had a wood cabinet to hold my accounts. I smoked. Tobacco was a means to relax. I sipped wine.

The province's stockpiles consisted of a season's crops. Our herds were reduced. Wild game supplemented our livestock. Wild rice was harvested. On the lakes formal warfare continued. Regular troops were employed. Once again Amherst attempted with his army to isolate Ticonderoga. He refrained from a direct assault. Montcalm attempted to envelop Amherst by Indian raid and maneuver. It was the autumn of 1758.

I was home. The war on the lakes continued. Montcalm's Indians were out of control. They were disciplined. Amherst preserved his flank and continued to isolate Ticonderoga.

Partisan warfare continued. I had news. My brother Half Huron was slain on Lake Champlain. I mourned him and consoled my family. Half Huron had been a Huron chief. I respected my half-brother.

At home I was at my desk. I worked my accounts. Provisioning our forces continued. There was powder and lead. The harvest had been good.

There was news from the Ohio Valley. The colonist General Forbes had occupied Fort Duquesne. He renamed the structure Fort Pitt. In England our chief foe was William Pitt. He was prime minister to George II. Pitt was capable. He directed campaigns in Europe, the West Indies, and India. He also had his eye on Canada. Amherst was his appointment, as was Wolfe. Wolfe was positioned at the approaches to the Saint Lawrence River. Montcalm commanded at Quebec.

PART IV
Pont Levis

CHAPTER 23

Winter

L eslie Esperier, brigadier. It was January in New York City. In the past year, I commanded two regiments of British troops. May I say that my two line regiments of colonists had been adopted by the British Army? My two regiments were Royal Americans.

While my troops drilled on the common in New York, I studied the strategy of former years. I had quarters in New York City. On the eastern shore of Lake George, General Amherst invested Ticonderoga. His army placed pressure on the French center.

In Nova Scotia General Wolfe was preparing to advance on Quebec. My Royal Americans were held in reserve in New York. In this year George II was old.

God bless the king. We had seen sedition. French espionage had inflamed the Jacobites. Charles Stuart, pretender to the throne, had been defeated at Culloden. In England the Duke of Cumberland, son of George II, had influence. Major Esperier had been made colonel and then was awarded the rank of general. I commanded a brigade. Light infantry were attached to my two line regiments.

I rented a house. I was a bachelor at sixty-nine. I had a valet and staff. I sipped a glass of wine. My study had shelves of books. I studied tactics as well. It was evening. A guest played the minuet. There was conversation.

"Are we included in Wolfe's advance on Quebec?" an orderly asked.

"Yes. I have orders for Nova Scotia," I said.

Wolfe had a high reputation. To others he wasn't liked. I liked General Wolfe. I had orders for the forthcoming campaign.

In trousers, with suspenders, I was in my shirt. I conversed easily. It was the beginning of a decisive year. We needed to obey. My regiments were good. Trained in frontier warfare, they drilled to stand in line. Discipline was stern. My Royal Americans were the Sixty-Second and Sixty-Fourth British Regiments. They faced in line of battle.

I relaxed. It was evening in New York City. In reflection I must discuss my years in New York. I had returned to England for a few years. The city was a bourg in its own right. Ships fitted the harbor from trade routes across the globe.

New York Bay saw sailing ships from Europe and the Orient. On Long Island and Manhattan the bourg flourished. From the Hudson Valley were foodstuffs. Manufactures and goods were traded aboard seagoing vessels.

I had seen the town grow up. From a hamlet at the turn of the century, the city swelled with populace and produce. On the common my two line regiments formed. The Sixty-Second and Sixty-Fourth would fall in—a parade.

Mounted on a thoroughbred, I observed the formations.

"Dismissed."

My men were uniformed in blue with crimson facings. They were shod in boots and wore tricorn hats. My two regiments with their colonels were imposing in line.

The men went to lunch. Beef and bread was their ration.

The troops, paid in shillings, were quartered in public buildings. As the men consumed their meal, I gave the order that they be let go for the day. I returned to my house.

Having previously rented, I purchased the house several years ago. It stood on a street near the harbor.

The previous summer, repulsed at Ticonderoga, Louisbourg had fallen. The English controlled the approaches to the Saint Lawrence River. An attack on Quebec was planned. Amherst faced Lake George with an army. Wolfe was ordered to take Quebec. On Ontario Fort Frontenac had also been taken. There was pressure from the west on the interior.

In my house I sat in my study. I wore slippers. A valet offered me a glass of claret. I sipped wine. I had a writing book to scribble orders.

I directed the equipment and discipline of two line regiments. Cartridges and a bayonet were issued. The troops mustered in. They were British regiments. Their uniform was prescribed by regulation. They were resplendent in indigo wool clothing faced in satin.

I commanded one thousand colonists. They were regular British troops. My valet refilled my glass. In younger years I had published several volumes of notes. Interest in *Notes on America* was read of. It was afternoon, an overcast day. The regiments had orders to campaign in the spring. The summer would see us in Nova Scotia.

[[missing page]]

CHAPTER 24

The Thaw

Let me describe New York City in the late 1750s. The city had become a port within several generations. Standing out to sea, its commerce traveled the Orient to India and home. The Levant was also a port of call.

I was home. It was March. My regiments drilled to the stern discipline exacted of them. Clad in indigo blue with white cross-belts, my Royal Americans stood as British troops. Sergeants issued orders as officers stood by.

I was home and drank wine. Madeira was good. I was alone at night. I poured wine. I relaxed. Within call was an orderly.

I was made busy. In Nova Scotia and on Cape Breton Island, Wolfe mobilized his army. Ten thousand regulars and additional seamen were being deployed. This was our thrust at the citadel of Quebec.

The French could muster five thousand regular troops with thousands of Canadians. The Royal Americans were to be included as part of Wolfe's army. Skirmishing and tactics with facing in line were taught.

Discipline was stern. I was pleased. I sipped wine. Port was good. My desk was busy. Maintaining and equipping two regiments was a task.

We embarked in May for Nova Scotia. I drilled my men.

The maneuver was to wheel left or guide right. They leveled their Brown Bess muskets with fixed bayonets, and on order a single volley was being ingrained.

I slept. I was up at 5:00 a.m. I breakfasted on tinned tongue. I drank a cup of tea. Munching a biscuit, I donned my uniform coat. The thaw had set in during March. It was now May. Having been transported by sea, we camped.

In the morning I observed my men falling in. A number of companies of fusiliers in scarlet coats were attached. The Royal Americans, thirteen hundred strong, stood inspection.

We camped on a sandbar, waiting to be ferried to the Saint Lawrence River. In my tent I studied the contingency plans of the campaign. Wolfe, with an army, advanced on Quebec by sea. Montcalm commanded in Quebec.

On our sandbar the men ate bully beef. It was noon. Grog was served. In the afternoon the men drilled. Maneuver and forming line was practiced. My sergeants were English Army cadre. My men rested. The campaign would be arduous. I sipped wine. Claret was poured. I instructed my colonels.

We were two battalions in Wolfe's army. The Royal Navy would escort us to Cape Breton. Quebec was a citadel of upper and lower towns. The French awaited us.

CHAPTER 26

Spring

It was May. I had packed a case of wine to be opened in Quebec. We had orders to move. Transports awaited us for Cape Breton Island. The Royal Americans were included in Wolfe's army. As regulars, Wolfe's army numbered nine thousand troops. Quebec was fortified. The Saint Lawrence River was heavily fortified. Twenty-two British gunships supported Wolfe. I finished my wine and gripped my small sword. My colonels were instructed.

Boarding began on the transports. A half regiment to a transport was done. A frigate would escort us to Nova Scotia. That afternoon at sea I could not describe the crowded transports. Within days we were landed in harbor in Nova Scotia. My Royal Americans pitched camp.

There were other British regiments. Coldstream and Gordon described them. A ranking general instructed me. My regiments were to bivouac until further notice. Raiding parties harassed us. The French and Indians took coup. My men were colonists and answered the French and Indians.

In camp I had my men assemble or stand in formation. Discipline was enforced. As regular troops, my men went to lunch. Beef was their ration. Once a month they drew their pay.

Weeks passed. It was summer. My men boarded lighters that transported them to the Saint Lawrence River. It was a week in

June. Quebec was situated on the Saint Lawrence River. The Île de Orléans lay amid the river. To either side of the stream were cliffs. Tributaries flowed into the river.

We were landed at the Montmorency River, a tributary to the Saint Lawrence. There were three enclaves surrounding Quebec, which was under siege. We opposed the French on the front of the Montmorency River. Pont Levis across the river from the town and Île de Orléans were also enclaves. The Royal Americans were in camp. I reported to my superiors. General Wolfe was pleased.

CHAPTER 27

Quebec Revisited

Our task was to invest Quebec. Having established enclave, our task was formidable. Quebec nestled on the Saint Charles River, a tributary of the Saint Lawrence. There was a lower town. On the height overlooking the lower town was the upper town. Cliffs surrounded the river. Opposite Quebec on the further shore was Pont Levis.

British artillery had been placed on Pont Levis. With heavy guns and mortars, the British bombarded Quebec. On the Montmorency River were British infantry. The terrain was against British troops. The Royal Americans were camped.

On the Île de Orléans were more British infantry. They put pressure on the lower town. Upon the Saint Lawrence River were fifty gunships and frigates bombarding the citadel of Quebec. The Marquis de Montcalm commanded the defense.

On the Montmorency the Royal Americans were entrenched. Musket fire was aimed at the woods. French and Indians harassed us. At night sentinels were found dead. It was the end of June. On Pont Levis, howitzers and mortars continued to bombard the upper town of Quebec.

General Wolfe surveyed the geography. He noted the cliffs.

There was activity on the Montmorency River. English regulars demonstrated. The Royal Americans trained English troops in frontier warfare. This was the situation in July. The Marquis de Montcalm surveyed the English. French provincials were drafted to supplement French regular troops.

Cannon fire rained on Quebec. The citadel of Quebec on its heights defied the English. General Montcalm was confident of his position. The English enclaves were isolated.

General Wolfe had naval support. He implored the fleet to force the river upstream. It was the middle of July when the fleet controlled the river upstream and downstream. Emphasis was placed on subduing the upper and lower towns of Quebec. General Wolfe surveyed the geography again. The cliffs were imposing. Pont Levis continued to bombard the upper town. On the river and on the Île de Orléans, batteries fired on the lower town. It was amid this perspective that the end of July came.

Wolfe had planned an assault on the Montmorency. The assault was repulsed. Wolfe was undaunted. He continued to put pressure on Quebec. It was early August.

CHAPTER 28

Île de Orléans

I was in camp with the Royal Americans. We were the Sixty-Second and Sixty-Fourth British Regiments. The Algonquian harassed us. French and Indians were in the woods. Our camp was fortified. Our howitzer was aimed at the woods. I inspected my men. They were grenadiers. Clad in indigo blue with cross-belts, the men had Brown Bess muskets. Accustomed to British Army tactics, the men stood in line. I was pleased.

Several companies of British light infantry were attached. Altogether, our complement of Royal Americans were nine hundred active duty. In camp I inspected my men. Wall tents were raised. In company I glanced at clean gaiters, blackened shoes or boots, and white collars. Muskets were inspected for clean bore, and pan, and flint. Bayonets were sharpened. I, General Esperier, had a wall tent. There was a table and a cot. I sat at the table and wrote orders.

The Algonquian were in earnest. Canadians could be seen. A picket line was placed in front of our fortified camp. It was thus we sat at lunch and ate salt beef. There was bread. Grog was issued. In my tent I ate bread and cheese and sipped wine.

My colonels reported. We were in good position. Snipers harassed us. A scalp lock was taken by the Algonquian. My men persevered. The attack at the end of July had been a failure. In the aftermath, the Royal Americans held the British flank. Thus it was August.

We maintained our position. British troops reinforced us.

The falls of the Montmorency were distant. In camp I enforced discipline. Morale was good. French regulars formed. We fired our howitzer. Weeks passed. Camp life was rigorous. The men stood in formation. The noon meal was served, salt beef with biscuit. A ration of grog was issued. Each month the men drew their pay, an English shilling. We had held on the Montmorency. It was toward September that I was issued orders: We must move to the Île de Orléans. We were being relieved.

We left our camps and entrenchments as we moved to the Saint Lawrence River. Barges carried us to the Île de Orléans. We slept on our packs. An operation was under way. We were told to be ready on the Île de Orléans.

Fires were forbidden. We ate cold biscuits. It was September. A day had passed. I stood with my men again. We had slept on our arms. Dusk approached. Movements on the river were masked. The Royal Americans boarded their longboats. Silence was imposed.

CHAPTER 29

Wolfe and Montcalm

It was the next morning. Forty-five hundred British troops were drawn up on the plains of Abraham. The French advanced in rolling volleys. I awaited the order to fire. The Sixty-Second and Sixty-Fourth British Regiments were in the line of battle. Word came to fire.

The French front disintegrated as the French broke and fled. Word came to advance. Word came that General Wolfe had fallen. Later we learned General Montcalm was mortally wounded too.

Wolfe was dead. General Montcalm would die the next day. The British armament had captured Quebec. That evening I unpacked the case of Madeira I had packed in New York. Montreal would surrender the following summer.

Printed in the United States
By Bookmasters